Leo the Lop
(tail three)

Written by: Stephen Cosgrove
Illustrated by: Robin James

A Serendipity Book

PRICE/STERN/SLOAN
Publishers, Inc., Los Angeles
1980

Copyright © 1980 by Serendipity Communications, Ltd.
Published by Price/Stern/Sloan Publishers, Inc.
410 North La Cienega Boulevard, Los Angeles, California 90048

Printed in the United States of America. All rights reserved. No part of this publication may
be reproduced, stored in a retrieval system, or transmitted, in any form or by any means,
electronic, mechanical, photocopying, recording, or otherwise, without the prior written
permission of the publishers.
ISBN: 0-8431-0577-1

Dedicated to Jennifer and Julie, my two beautiful daughters who get bored on cloudy days.

Their Father

The snow fell lightly and brought the quiet hush of winter to the forest. With each passing day, more and more snow fell until everything was covered in a soft and gentle blanket.

The creatures of the forest were nestled warmly in their beds, sleeping away the cares of winter and dreaming of a warm summer morning.

All of the creatures, that is, except for a fuzzy, flop-eared rabbit named Leo, who was bored stiff. It wasn't that Leo was always bored but with the coming of winter he had to stay indoors more and more because it was cold and wet outside.

Leo searched in vain for something to do. He dug out a musty old game and tried to play it by himself. Now we all know that playing a game by yourself sometimes can be really boring, so, sadly he put the game away. Leo tried making funny faces in the mirror but even that didn't make him happy.

"There's nothing to do!" he sighed to himself. "And I'm so bored."

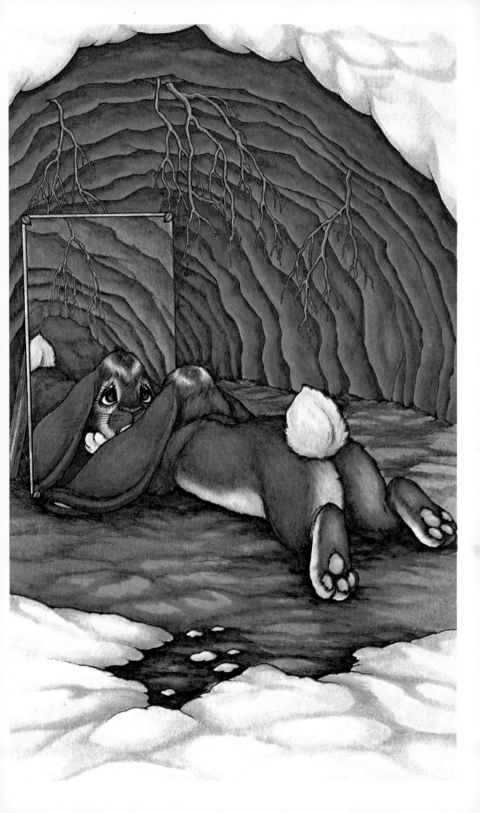

"I know!" he shouted in glee, to no one in particular. "I'll go outside and find somebody to play with!" With that he wrapped himself up in his favorite scarf, put on his mittens and dashed happily out into the snow. He looked and looked but could find no one to play with.

"Where is everybody?" he thought. Then suddenly, it dawned on him. "They must have gone to sleep for the winter. Well, I just go wake them up!" So off he hopped through the fluffy drifts of snow.

Leo slipped and slid over to an old weathered oak tree and carefully climbed up to a crook on the main branch. There, just as he had remembered from last summer, was the hole where the squirrels lived. He knocked softly on the tree and quietly said, "Oh squirrels... Wake up! It's boring out here and I want to play with someone."

He listened very carefully but the only thing he heard was soft snoring and somebody mumbling in their sleep.

"They probably didn't hear me" Leo thought. "Come on squirrels!" he shouted, as he pounded on the tree. "It's time to wake up and play!"

Well, the squirrels heard him that time, for Leo could hear them rustling about grumbling and muttering.

"What's going on?" yawned a sleepy and very upset squirrel as he joined Leo on the limb.

"I was bored!" said Leo with a big smile on his face. "So, I thought I'd wake you guys up and we could play some games or something."

The squirrel looked at him in disbelief. "You woke us up so you could play some stupid game?" he shouted. With a puff and a snort, he shoved Leo off the tree and sent him flying into the snowbank below. "Silly rabbit! Go find somebody else to play with. It's cold outside and we need our sleep." With a yawn and a stretch, he shuffled back into the warm comfort of the tree.

Leo sat in the snow for a moment or two as he tried to understand what had happened. "Dumb old squirrel. Probably got up on the wrong side of bed." He looked around trying to figure out who else he could play with when, suddenly, he spied a flock of little birds flitting about.

"Hi, birds!" he shouted. "I'm bored and don't have anything to do. Do you want to play?" The birds landed on a branch right above Leo and looked at him curiously. "Are you kidding?" they said. "We're looking for food and you want to know if we want to play? You must be nuts!" And with that they flew away in a flutter of feathers.

Leo was becoming very confused. He was bored. There was nothing to do and no one to do it with even if he could find something to do. "Oh, pooh!" he grumbled as he kicked the snow out of his way.

He wandered about aimlessly for hours and hours looking in vain for something to do when the winter's silence was broken by a voice out of nowhere: "Who are you and what are you doing?"

Leo turned around trying to find who had spoken and finally he looked up into the snowy branches and saw an old owl. "My name is Leo," he sighed, "and I was so bored staying in my den that I thought I would wake somebody up to play with. The squirrels were too tired, and the birds were too busy and I'm bored stiff!"

The owl thought for a moment or two and then quietly said, "Did you ever stop to think that maybe you could play by yourself and have just as much fun?"

Leo scratched his ear with his big thumpy foot and sputtered, "But there's nothing to do and no one to share things with!"

"Well, there's lots of things to do," said the owl, "and after you've done them, come this spring you can tell all your friends about your marvelous winter fun."

"Well, I'll try," said Leo as he started to walk away. Suddenly, with a smile on his face he turned and asked, "Uh, do you want to play?"

"No, Leo. I too have to find food to eat and you must learn to entertain yourself." And with that the owl flew away leaving Leo sitting in the snow all alone.

"Well," he sighed, "I guess I've got to try!" And try he did. He walked all over the forest looking for something to do but there didn't seem to be anything there. He walked up the hills through the heavy snow searching and searching.

"I'm getting tired of hopping through the snow. Maybe I'll just slide down the hill and go home." He sat back on his big feet and slid quickly down the hill.

"Hmmmm!" he said brightly. "That was kind of fun." So, he found a bigger hill and climbed to the top. This time, with a little bit of a jump, he began swooshing down the hill faster and faster zigging this way and that.

"Wow! That is fun." And he continued to slide for an hour or more.

Finally Leo got a little tired and thought, "Maybe there are more things I can do myself."

He looked around and decided what he could do. He rolled a ball of snow, then several more, put them all together and built the biggest snow bunny that had ever been built in the forest. Boy, was that fun!

Leo went home late that afternoon a tired but very happy rabbit.

He played like this for days and days. Building snow bunnies, sliding down the hills, and once or twice he just laid in the snow waving his arms making funny figures.

As he was playing like this one morning, he noticed a small green shoot peeping through the snow. He looked around and sure enough there were little shoots all over the place.

"It must be the beginning of spring!" he shouted gleefully.

Sure enough, Leo had been having so much fun he didn't even know that spring had sprung. As he watched in quiet amazement, the flowers began to bloom and the snow softly melted.

Leo spent most of the spring and part of the summer telling the other creatures about the wonderful time he had during the winter, playing by himself. By telling them of his adventures, it was almost as if they spent the winter playing with him.

And though he played with all the animals whenever he could, once in a while Leo would go off alone and play by himself.

SO, WHEN YOU'RE ALL ALONE AND
THERE IS NOTHING TO DO
REMEMBER LEO'S LESSON FOR
YOU CAN ALWAYS PLAY WITH YOU

Serendipity Books

Written by
Stephen Cosgrove

Illustrated by
Robin James

In Search of the Saveopotomas   The Gnome From Nome
The Muffin Muncher   The Wheedle on the Needle
Serendipity   The Dream Tree
Jake O'Shawnasey   Hucklebug
Morgan and Me   Creole
Flutterby   Bangalee
Nitter Pitter   Catundra
Leo The Lop   Cap'n Smudge
Leo The Lop-Tail Two   Maui-Maui
Leo The Lop-Tail Three   Little Mouse on the Prairie
Snaffles   Shimmeree
Kartusch   Trafalgar True

$1.50 each

Boxed Sets Nos. 1, 2, 3, 4
(5 books in each set) $7.50 per set

Serendipity Books are available wherever books are sold
or may be obtained from the publisher by sending price of book
or boxed set, plus 50 cents for handling and mailing.

PRICE/STERN/SLOAN *Publishers, Inc.*
410 North La Cienega Boulevard, Los Angeles, California 90048